TOYS GO OUT

❖

BEING THE ADVENTURES

OF A KNOWLEDGEABLE STINGRAY,

A TOUGHY LITTLE BUFFALO,

AND SOMEONE CALLED PLASTIC

❖

EMILY JENKINS

ILLUSTRATED BY PAUL O. ZELINSKY

❖

A YEARLING BOOK

Text copyright © 2006 by Emily Jenkins
Illustrations copyright © 2006 by Paul O. Zelinsky
All rights reserved. Published in the United States by Yearling, an imprint of Random House Children's Books, a division of Penguin Random House LLC, New York. Originally published in hardcover by Schwartz & Wade Books, an imprint of Random House Children's Books, New York, in 2006.

Yearling and the jumping horse design are registered trademarks of Penguin Random House LLC.

Visit us on the Web! randomhousekids.com
Educators and librarians, for a variety of teaching tools, visit us at RHTeachersLibrarians.com

The Library of Congress has cataloged the hardcover edition of this work as follows:
Jenkins, Emily.
Toys go out : being the adventures of a knowledgeable Stingray, a toughy little Buffalo, and someone called Plastic / Emily Jenkins ; illustrated by Paul O. Zelinsky.—1st ed.
p. cm.
Summary: Six stories relate the adventures of three best friends, who happen to be toys.
ISBN 978-0-375-83604-6 (hardcover) — ISBN 978-0-375-93604-3 (lib. bdg.) —
ISBN 978-0-307-56073-5 (ebook)
[1. Toys—Fiction. 2. Best friends—Fiction. 3. Friendship—Fiction.
4. Adventure and adventurers—Fiction.] I. Zelinsky, Paul O., ill. II. Title.
PZ7.J4134Toy 2006
[E]—dc22
2005022431

ISBN 978-0-385-73661-9 (pbk.)

Printed in the United States of America
40 39 38 37 36 35 34
First Yearling Edition 2008

With great thanks to Anne Schwartz,

my editor, who saw a light in my little manuscript

that took place entirely in the dark

—E.J.

For Radish Bedundt and his ilk

—P.Z.

CONTENTS

✣

IN THE BACKPACK, WHERE IT IS VERY DARK

1

THE SERIOUS PROBLEM OF PLASTIC-NESS

13

THE TERRIFYING BIGNESS OF THE WASHING MACHINE

35

THE POSSIBLE SHARK

57

HOW LUMPHY GOT ON THE BIG HIGH BED AND LOST
SOMETHING RATHER GOOD-LOOKING

79

IT IS DIFFICULT TO FIND THE RIGHT BIRTHDAY PRESENT

101

CHAPTER ONE

❧

In the Backpack,
Where It Is Very Dark

The backpack is dark and smells like a wet bathing suit.

Waking up inside, Lumphy feels cramped and grumped. "I wish I had been asked," he moans. "If I had been asked, I would have said I wasn't going."

"Shhh," says StingRay, though she doesn't like the dark backpack any more than Lumphy. "It's not so bad if you don't complain."

"We weren't told about this trip," snorts Lumphy. "We were just packed in the night."

"Why don't you shut your buffalo mouth?" snaps StingRay. "Your buffalo mouth is far too whiny."

There is a small nip on the end of her tail, and StingRay curls it away from Lumphy's big square buffalo teeth.

Plastic usually hums when she is feeling nervous. "Um tum tum—um tum tum—tum—tiddle—tee," she trills, to see if it will make the inside of the backpack seem any nicer.

"Don't you know the words to that song?" asks Lumphy.

"There are no words. It's a hum," answers Plastic.

No one says anything for a while, after that.

"Does anyone know where we're going in here?" wonders Lumphy.

Plastic does not.

StingRay doesn't, either.

"My stomach is uncomfortable," grumphs the buffalo. "I think I'm going to be sick."

· · · · ·

Buh-buh bump! It feels like the backpack is going down some stairs. Or maybe up some stairs.

Or maybe up something worse than stairs.

StingRay tries to think calming thoughts. She pictures the high bed with the fluffy pillows where she usually sleeps. She pictures the Little Girl with the blue barrette, who scratches where the ears would be if StingRay had ears. But none of these thoughts makes her feel calm.

"I hope we're not going to the vet," StingRay says, finally.

"What's the vet?" asks Lumphy.

"The vet is a big human dressed in a white coat who puts animals in a contraption made from rubber bands, in order to see what is wrong with them," answers StingRay, who sometimes says she knows things when she doesn't. "Then he pokes them over and over

with needles the size of carrots,

and makes them drink nasty-tasting medicine,

and puts them in the bumpity washing

machine to fix whatever's broken."

"If anyone needs to go to the vet, it's the one-eared sheep," says Plastic, remembering the oldest of the Little Girl's toys. "And Sheep's not even here. No, we can't be going to the vet. We aren't broken."

"Speak for yourself," snorts Lumphy, who feels even sicker than before at the thought of the bumpity washing machine.

. . . . .

Woosh. Woosh. The backpack begins to swing.

Back and forth. Back and forth.

Or maybe round and round.

"I hope we're not going to the zoo," moans StingRay.

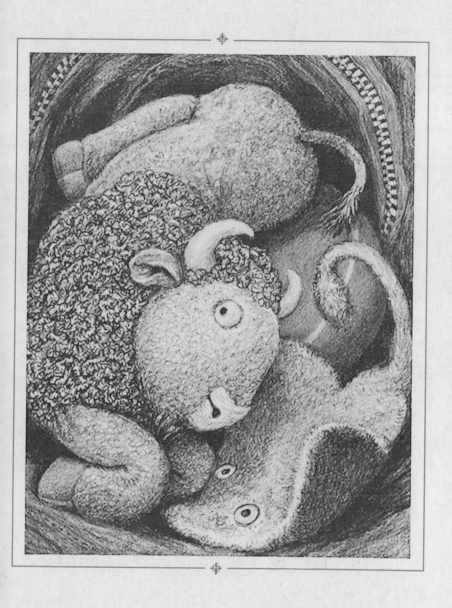

"They'll put us in cages with no one to talk to. Each one in a separate cage,

and we'll have to woosh back and forth all day,

and do tricks on giant swings,

with people throwing quarters at our faces,

and teasing."

"I don't think we're big enough for the zoo," Plastic says hopefully. "I'm pretty sure they're only interested in very large animals over there."

"I'm large," says Lumphy.

"She means really, really, very large," says StingRay. "At the zoo they have stingrays the size of choo-choo trains;

and plastics the size of swimming pools.

Zoo buffaloes would never fit in a backpack.

They eat backpacks for lunch, those

buffaloes."

"Is that true?" asks Lumphy, but nobody answers him.

. . . . .

Plunk! The backpack is thrown onto the ground.

Or maybe into a trash can.

Or onto a garbage truck.

"We might be going to the dump!" cries StingRay. "We'll be tossed in a pile of old green beans,

and sour milk cartons,

because the Little Girl doesn't love us

anymore,

and it will be icy cold all the time,

and full of garbage-eating sharks,

and it will smell like throw-up."

"I don't think so," soothes Plastic.

"I'll be forced to sleep on a slimy bit of used paper baggie, instead of on the big high bed with the fluffy pillows!" continues StingRay.

There is a noise outside the backpack. Not a big noise, but a rumbly one. "Did you hear that?" asks StingRay. "I think it is the X-ray machine. The vet is going to X-ray us one by one

and look into our insides with an enormous

magnifying glass,

and then poke us with the giant carrot!"

"I'm sure it's not an X-ray," says Plastic calmly, although she isn't sure at all. "An X-ray would be squeakier."

"Then I think it is a lion," cries StingRay. "A lion at the zoo who does not want to be on display with any small creatures like you and me.

A lion who doesn't like sharing her swing set,

and wants all the quarters for herself.

She is roaring because she hasn't had any

lunch yet,

and her favorite food is stingrays."

"A lion would be fiercer," says Plastic, a bit uncertainly. "It would sound hungrier, I bet."

"Maybe it is a giant buffalo," suggests Lumphy.

"Maybe it is a dump truck!" squeals StingRay. "A big orange dump truck tipping out piles of rotten groceries on top of us,

> and trapping us with the garbage-eating
>
> sharks
>
> and the throw-up smell!"

"Wouldn't a dump truck be louder?" asks Plastic, though she is starting to think StingRay might have a point. "I'm sure it's not a dump truck."

. . . . .

The backpack thumps down again with a bang. "I would like to be warned," moans Lumphy. "Sudden bumps make everything worse than it already is."

"The Girl doesn't love us and she's trying to get rid of us!" cries StingRay in a panic.

The backpack opens. The rumbly noise gets louder,

and the light is very bright—so bright that StingRay, Plastic, and Lumphy have to squinch up their eyes and take deep breaths before they can see where they are. A pair of warm arms takes them all out of the dark, wet-bathing-suit smell together.

The three toys look around. There are small chairs, a sunny window, and a circle of fidgety faces.

It is not the vet.

It is not the zoo.

It is not the dump. (They are pretty sure.)

But where is it?

The rumbly noise surges up. A grown-up asks everyone to Please Be Quiet Now. And then comes a familiar voice.

"These are my best friends," says the Little Girl who owns the backpack and sleeps in the high bed with the fluffy pillows. "My best friends in the world. That's why I brought them to show-and-tell."

"Welcome," says the teacher.

Sticky, unfamiliar fingers pat Lumphy's head and StingRay's plush tail.

Plastic is held up for all to admire. "We are here to be shown and told," she whispers to StingRay and Lumphy, feeling quite bouncy as she looks around at the schoolroom. "Not to be thrown away or put under the X-ray machine!"

The teacher says Lumphy looks a lot like a real buffalo. (Lumphy wonders what the teacher means by "real," but he is too happy to worry much about it.)

"We're special!" whispers StingRay. "We're her best friends!"

"I knew it would be something nice," says Plastic.

. . . . .

Funny, but the ride home is not so uncomfortable. The smell is still there, but the backpack seems rather cozy. Plastic has herself a nap.

StingRay isn't worried about vets and zoos and garbage dumps anymore; she curls herself into a ball by Lumphy's buffalo stomach. "The Little Girl loves us," she tells him. "I knew it all along, really. I just didn't want to say."

Lumphy licks StingRay's head once, and settles down to wait. When he knows where he is going, traveling isn't so bad. And right now, he is going home.

CHAPTER TWO

❧

The Serious Problem
of Plastic-ness

The room with the high bed and the fluffy pillows has bookshelves. Plastic never paid much attention to them before, but now she thinks they are interesting. Most of the shelves hold storybooks, but the bottom one has schoolbooks on it: books about animals, the meanings of words, the size of oceans, and the ways of plants.

"When you've been to school like I have," says StingRay, interrupting one evening as Plastic is looking curiously at the shelves, "—when you've gone to show-and-tell and seen the classroom and all the important things they have in there, then you know that books are a place to find out truths."

"Truths about what?" asks Plastic.

"Just truths," says StingRay, positioning herself proudly in front of the books. "Like what is two and two?"

"Four," pipes up Lumphy, who is watching the sun set from the windowsill nearby.

"If we want the answer," explains StingRay, as if she hasn't heard him, "we can look it up. Truths like these are in books. That's what you learn at school, if you've been to school like I have."

"We were *all* at school," mutters Lumphy, still on the windowsill.

Plastic wants to know which book would have that truth inside, about two and two.

"A book on money," says StingRay. "It tells you how to be rich and famous

and how to fill up your really big swimming

pool with liquid gold,

and how to eat expensive chocolates for

breakfast,

and have banquets for hundreds of your best

friends,

and swing from chandeliers made from

diamonds.

Also, how to count numbers together, if that is the kind of truth you are after."

"How is that a truth?" calls Lumphy.

"Okay, a fact, then. Facts are in books. If you've been to school."

"Ahem," coughs Lumphy. "I was right there next to you. Don't you remember?"

"Where?"

"At school."

"Time for bed," StingRay says importantly.

The Little Girl comes into the bedroom and lifts her up to sleep on the high bed with the fluffy pillows, while Lumphy and Plastic stay where they are.

. . . . .

"Let's find the book on money," suggests Plastic, when the lights are out and both StingRay and the Girl are asleep.

Lumphy makes a grouchy noise. Now that it's night and the Girl can't see him moving around, he wants to go down the hall to visit TukTuk, the yellow towel who lives in the bathroom. TukTuk always has something interesting to say. She sees a lot of strange behavior in her life as a towel, although she doesn't get out much. Lumphy particularly likes to hear about tooth brushing and fingernail clipping, things he is not sure he properly understands. "I'm busy," he tells Plastic.

So Plastic tries to get the one-eared sheep to look for the money book.

"Is there anything about grass in it?" Sheep wants to know.

"I don't think so. It's the truths and facts of liquid gold swimming pools."

"Anything about clover?"

"Probably not," Plastic is forced to admit.

"If it's not going to be interesting, I'd just as soon skip it," Sheep says kindly. She goes to play marbles with the toy mice.

Plastic looks at the books by herself, reading the titles on the spines. One explains the meanings of words. One is full of maps. Another is about the wonderful world of plants. But there isn't any book on money or gold swimming pools—and even if there was one, Plastic couldn't pull it out from the shelf.

Only one book lies open on the floor so that she can read it: a book about animals, with pictures and details about how they live, what they eat, and where they sleep at night.

Plastic finds the part about stingrays. They live in the ocean and flap their flipper-wings like birds in the sky. She reads about sheep and how their woolly coats get shorn. She reads about mice, who are part of the rodent family. And she reads a good deal about buffaloes and how they run around in herds.

"Ooh," she realizes. "I can read about plastics!"

But plastics aren't there.

She looks again.

They still aren't there.

Then Plastic goes page by page through the animal book, looking at every picture of every single animal.

None of them looks like her.

Ladybugs are round and red, but Plastic doesn't have wings like a ladybug.

Turtles are round when their legs are inside their shells, but Plastic does not have a hard shell, or any kind of shell at all.

Hedgehogs are round when they curl themselves in balls, but Plastic is not spiny like a hedgehog.

People say foxes are red—but really they are much more orange, and anyway, Plastic knows she is not a fox. She is not sure she even has a nose.

Where are the plastics? she wonders, and calls the toy mice over to help her pull out the book on the meanings of words. The mice skitter off as soon as they are done, leaving Plastic alone with the book. It is called a Dictionary.

She finds the P's, and reads: "Plastic. A material produced by polymeri-something-or-other" (a very long word).

But where do we live? wonders Plastic. *What do we like to eat?*

She reads on. "Plastic. Capable of being shaped or formed. Also, artificial."

Plastic doesn't know what Artificial means, so she looks that up, too. "Fake," says the dictionary. "Not natural."

Artificial doesn't sound nice at all.

Plastic scoots under the high bed and doesn't come out for several hours.

· · · · ·

When he gets back from visiting TukTuk the towel, Lumphy finds Plastic and crawls under the bed next to her. "Did you know the Little Girl puts a piece of waxy

string in between her teeth every night before bed?" he asks. "It's called dental floss."

No, Plastic didn't know.

"I wouldn't want string between my teeth," says Lumphy.

Plastic is not sure she even has teeth.

"Especially not with wax."

"Maybe it feels nice," suggests Plastic. "You never know until you try."

"I know without trying."

"Could it be a cleaning thing? Since she does it in the bathroom."

"Nah," says Lumphy. "What could you clean with a piece of string?"

Plastic doesn't know.

"All this cleaning, I don't see what it's about, anyway," Lumphy adds.

Plastic tells Lumphy about the dictionary and how it says that plastics are Artificial.

"Hmmm." Lumphy scratches his ear and turns around three times in the spot where he plans to sleep. "You don't say what you really think," he says, finally. "You pretend everything's all right when it isn't."

"So?"

"So, that's artificial."

"What about polymeri-something-or-other?"

Lumphy curls himself into a ball. "It's too late to discuss big words." He closes his eyes.

Plastic is the tiniest bit angry. "*Real* buffaloes are interested in other people's problems," she says. "*Real* buffaloes don't sleep when someone is talking to them. I read it in a book."

Lumphy lifts his head. His face looks nervous. "What do you mean, *real* buffaloes?"

Suddenly, Plastic feels like she isn't being very nice. And whatever plastics are, she wants to be a good one. "Nothing," she answers. "Never mind."

. . . . .

"I need to know the truth about plastics," Plastic confesses to StingRay the next morning, as they are sunning themselves in a square of light on the shaggy rug. "I can't find it in a book."

"What do you need to know?" asks StingRay kindly. "I'm sure I can answer."

"Their natural habitat," says Plastic. "And what they eat; and whether they are birds, or fish, or mammals."

"Mammals, definitely," answers StingRay, who doesn't actually know. "They're very furry, plastics. And their natural habitat is the frozen tundra,

where icicles grow up from the ground,

and the wind whistles,

and it's dark thirty hours a day in winter.

The plastics live in igloos that they build with

their teeth,

and they eat whale meat and also seals and

walruses that they catch,

and swallow whole.

Does that help?

I think it's a pretty thorough answer."

"Yes, thank you," says Plastic, with a bit of a sniffle. "I just wonder," she mentions. "I'm not very furry."

"You probably lost your fur in an accident," says StingRay. "It doesn't look bad at all, though. Really."

Plastic tries to remember a fur-losing accident, but it must have slipped her mind.

. . . . .

After seven hours in front of the television, Plastic is as confused as ever. She has watched four cooking shows, two soap operas, endless commercials, and one after-school special. She knows that there are plastic cups, forks, and containers; that these things are useful for taking on picnics and freezing leftover stew; and that a delightful tofu marinade can be made with only six ingredients. She also knows there are plastic toys ("May contain small plastic parts," the commercials say, "not suitable for children under three") and plastic garbage bags.

But she hasn't seen any of the plastics eating whale meat, or living in igloos, or growing fur—though maybe the fur is hard to see on the small television screen. In any case, all the plastics look different. Most of them aren't even red. There isn't any herd, like there are herds of buffaloes. The Plastics don't build dams, or collect pollen, or live in tunnels. They *do* appear to be famous—and yet there are no plastics to whom Plastic feels connected. None of them seem to have anything in common besides their plastic-ness.

Which isn't much.

．．．．．

For four days and four nights, Plastic feels un-bouncy. She doesn't play marbles with the one-eared sheep; she doesn't make jokes with the rocking horse in the corner; and she doesn't play I Doubt It with Lumphy or checkers with StingRay. She looks out the window by herself and thinks about plastic-ness.

On the fifth night, Plastic remembers TukTuk. The towel knows about dental floss and fingernail clippers. Maybe she knows about plastics, too.

Plastic has only met TukTuk once before, and she feels embarrassed as she creeps down the hall and stops outside the bathroom door. Maybe TukTuk will not want a visit from a small, confused plastic. After all, she is used to large and furry friends like Lumphy.

But Plastic can't go on anymore, staring out the window, doing nothing all night.

Slowly, she enters the bathroom.

TukTuk is lying in a pile. The night-light in the bathroom glows a comforting pink, and the air is still warm from the Little Girl's bath.

"Excuse my appearance," says TukTuk, who can't get around on her own. "Plastic, isn't it? I'm always like this after the bath. Damp. On the floor. I'd like an iron and a fold, but this disarray is all that can be managed. Glad to see you nonetheless."

Plastic begins to cry. TukTuk seems like everything a towel should be. So nice, so floppy, and just so . . . so very towelly.

"Oh, Plastic!" soothes TukTuk. "There, there. Come, wipe yourself on my corner. I don't mind."

Plastic has a good long cry, and feels a little better. "I'm a rotten plastic," she sniffs to TukTuk. "I've lost my fur. I don't know my habitat, or my eating habits, or whether I build a nest or run in a herd. I'm not even sure I like what plastics *are*, anyway."

A big tear rolls onto the bathroom tile, and she begins mumbling about Fake, Artificial, and polymeri-something-or-other.

"Oh, my dear," comforts TukTuk. "You're upset about nothing."

"It's not nothing! It's plastic-ness!"

"Listen. I have something to tell you."

"You do?"

"It's important. Are you ready?"

Plastic thinks she is.

"You are not a plastic."

"I'm not?" Plastic isn't sure if she is happy or un-.

"Plastic is just your name," says TukTuk. "It's obvious, to anyone who knows anything, precisely what you are."

"It is?"

"Of course. You are a rubber ball."

"I am?"

"I've seen balls before you, I'll see balls after you. A ball is what you are," says TukTuk. "Tell me, do you bounce?"

"Yes!" cries Plastic. "I do!" And she bounces once, very high, for show.

"And do you roll?"

"Yes!" Plastic rolls around the bathroom until she crashes into the base of the toilet.

"And have you got front legs and back legs?"

"Um, not exactly," says Plastic, who most certainly doesn't have any.

"And no fur whatsoever?"

"No."

"That's normal for a ball, you know."

"What about how I don't have very much nose?"

"You mean, how you don't have *any* nose?"

"Um . . . yes," says Plastic.

"That's normal, too," explains TukTuk.

Plastic feels relieved.

"I have been around a long time," says TukTuk. "And I have never seen a ball with fur, or legs, or a nose. You're a ball, Plastic," says the towel, wrapping her terry-cloth corners around her friend. "Don't let anyone tell you different."

"I'm a ball!" cries Plastic. "A ball, ball, ball!"

Suddenly, she feels bouncy again. Really, really bouncy. She jumps in the tub and rolls around super-fast. She bounces herself so high she hits the ceiling. "A ball!"

"Enough, now. I need a rest," says TukTuk.

"All right." Plastic stops bouncing for a second and gives the towel a kiss.

Then she goes rolling,

bouncing,

rolling,

bouncing,

bounce, bounce, bouncing

down the hall to the bedroom.

CHAPTER THREE

❧

The Terrifying Bigness
of the Washing Machine

Lumphy has peanut butter on him. Here is how it happened.

He went on a picnic! The Little Girl and her father walked to a park, where there was a big pond and lots of grass and sunshine. The Girl carried Lumphy all the way there, holding on to his tail (it didn't hurt), and then they all three sat on a patchwork blanket and ate peanut butter and jam sandwiches, round green apples, and dried pineapple. They threw rocks into the pond.

Then the sky turned dark and it started to rain. The Girl and her father ran home as fast as they could, with Lumphy in the picnic basket.

The lid of the peanut butter jar was not on tight. Lumphy jounced and joggled and got goo all across his face and front legs. It was very greasy. When they arrived home, the Girl wiped him with a paper napkin, but he is still a very peanut-buttery buffalo.

The father says Lumphy will have to be washed.

"I don't see what the problem is," says Lumphy to StingRay, later that evening. The Little Girl is out for Chinese food with her parents, and the two of them are building block towers on the shaggy rug.

"You're dirty," says StingRay, placing a block on top of her pile.

"It's not dirt. It's food."

"Food *is* dirt when it's mashed in your fur."

"No it isn't. It's food. Why would it be dirt in your fur, but nice and tasty anywhere else?"

"It would be dirt if it was on the rug," says StingRay. "Or on the sofa."

"Food isn't dirty, or you wouldn't eat it. I have some nice clean food on me. I don't see that it's a problem that needs washing."

"If people think it's dirty, then it is," StingRay claims.

Plastic rolls by on her way to visit the rocking horse in the corner. "People bigger than you," she chimes in. "If people bigger than you think it's dirty—that's when it is."

"Clean is better than dirty," explains StingRay. "Like neat is better than messy,

> and smart is better than stupid,
>
> and chocolate is better than lentils,
>
> and blue is better than orange."

"I like orange," mutters Lumphy.

"Some people do," allows StingRay, lining up her blocks in a neat row. "But blue is better."

Lumphy does not want to be washed, especially after what TukTuk told him earlier about the bumpity washing machine in the basement—how you go round and round in soapy water, and how it makes you dizzy and sick to your stomach.

Lumphy asks StingRay if she knows anything about washing machines.

"Not from personal experience," StingRay admits. She is "dry clean only" and has never gotten wet. But she has a lot to say about basements. "They are dark and full of rats," she explains. "And there are spiders in the corners with fifty-eight legs,

> and ghosts hide there when the attic is full up,
>
> and there are cardboard boxes that anything
>
> could pop out of,

like sharks, or knives, or axe murderers,

and more dust than you ever saw in your life.

I don't know why you would go to a basement to get clean," muses StingRay. "Because basements are dirty places."

. . . . .

That night, Lumphy tells Plastic and StingRay he'll be going away for a while. He keeps his planned hiding place top-secret, even from his friends. He doesn't want to take any chances of being discovered.

Then he creeps into the closet, squeezing himself back behind a shoe box on the floor. He figures that if the Little Girl doesn't see him for a few weeks, she'll forget all about washing him. When he emerges from the closet he'll still be greasy—but she'll think that's just the way he is, not anything that needs to change.

"I am a greasy buffalo," he says to himself, and it sounds pretty tough.

For three days, he waits in the closet with only dust and socks for company. He hopes his peanutty smell doesn't give him away.

He waits . . .

and waits . . .

and waits.

He does not come out, even when the Little Girl is at school or asleep, because what if she came home early or woke up from a nightmare? He can't risk it.

He is lonely, all by himself in the closet.

One day, the Little Girl is searching for a particular pair of socks. She opens the door and begins rummaging right near where Lumphy is hiding. She's moving shoes and boxes and other bits of clutter. "Peanut butter," she says to her mother. "What smells like peanut butter?"

Lumphy dives headfirst into a soccer shoe. It is muddy from the Girl's practice the day before. He's too big for it, and has to scrunch his head all the way down into the toe in order to hide. Even then, his bottom is sticking out pretty far, and he is so worried about being found that his tail wags back and forth without him doing it on purpose.

He holds his breath and tries to stop his tail.

It won't stop.

He tries to squeeze his bottom in, so it won't be sticking out.

It won't squeeze.

He tries not to smell like peanut butter.

But he stinks.

The Little Girl roots around in the closet for eight days. Well, it is really eight minutes, but it

feels

like

eight

days

to Lumphy.

Finally, finally, finally, the Girl finds her particular sock and goes away.

Lumphy tries to get out.

He wiggles. He woggles.

He grunts, and humphs, and pushes.

But he's still in the shoe, with his bottom sticking out.

"Help!" he yells, but he is too deep in for anyone to hear him.

It is a long day. And a long night. Stuck in the shoe.

Around 4 a.m., the one-eared sheep wanders into the closet, following an interesting smell that she smells. Lumphy can tell it is her, because she makes a snorty noise when she walks. "What are you doing in there?" Sheep wants to know.

"Hrmmphle wurrffle," says Lumphy.

"Come out. I can't hear you."

"Wurrffle wummpffle!"

"What? Sorry," says the sheep. "It's my ear. I've lost it."

"Wurrffle wummpffle purrmple!"

Sheep doesn't understand. She is distracted by the tasty-looking lace of the soccer shoe. It's not grass, and it's not clover, but it looks pretty chewable to the sheep.

She settles down next to the shoe and has herself a lovely munch, pulling the lace out bit by bit. She hears a Wurrffle Wummmpffle noise, and it's irritating, but she doesn't let it bother her. Pretty soon the sound quiets down to nothing.

When she is done chewing the lace, Sheep is mildly surprised to find herself in the closet. She burps and goes out to play pick-up sticks with the toy mice.

· · · · ·

Two hours later, Lumphy (who fell asleep wedged in the dampness of the soccer shoe) wakes up to find he can lift his head. The lace has been chewed into fourteen small pieces, and without it, the shoe flops open. Lumphy waggles his shoulders and stands up. Then he steps gingerly out, and creeps into the bedroom to find the one-eared sheep dozing on the rug.

"Thanks," he whispers, nuzzling her woolly face. "You're a true friend."

Sheep has no idea what he is talking about.

Just then, the Little Girl rolls over and makes a mumbly noise. She is waking up!

Rumpa lumpa, rumpa lumpa—Lumphy gallops at top speed and dives behind the rocking horse in the corner.

The Girl stands and puts on her clothes. Then she begins looking around—under the bed, behind the bookshelf, even in the back of the closet, where Lumphy used to be hiding!

She's searching the room as if she's lost something,

rooting through the toy shelf, tossing whirly tops and colored markers and board games and mice every which way.

Then Lumphy hears a sad sound. He has heard it before, but not often. The Little Girl is crying. "He's not here!" she wails. "I need him!"

Lumphy peeks through the legs of the rocking horse so he can see the Girl's face. Her cheeks are wet.

"Lumphy, Lumphy!" The Girl throws herself on the bed, buries her face in the pillow, and weeps.

She misses me, Lumphy realizes. *She thinks I'm gone forever.*

The idea had never occurred to him.

He rushes out from behind the horse.

Ag! He remembers the washing machine and runs back behind the horse's legs.

Ag! The Little Girl is *crying*! Out again.

Ag! The washer. Back behind the legs.

Crying!

Out.

Washer!

Back.

Cry!

Wash!

Out!

Back!

Ag!

Lumphy cannot stand it anymore. He loves the Little Girl and he hates to make her cry. So although he is desperately afraid of the washing machine—and of the deep, dark basement with its ghosts, and rats, and axe murderers—he creeps out from behind the horse while the Little Girl is sobbing into her pillow.

Quietly, Lumphy tips over one of the green rubber boots sitting near the foot of the bed. Then he lies down (very cleverly) right in front of the boot, as if he'd been shoved down in there and only spilled out when the boot tipped over.

When the Girl stops crying and looks around for a tissue, she sees Lumphy lying there. She picks him up and kisses him all over his peanut-buttery face, squeezing him until he thinks his buffalo teeth might fall out. "Lumphy!" she cries. "You were in my boot!" She pets his head. "How did you get in my boot, you sweetie sweetie?"

For a moment, life is wonderful. Lumphy is happy.

Then the Girl smells him.

"You stink like peanut butter," she says. "And you're greasy. But don't worry, Lumphy. I know just what to do about *that*."

. . . . .

The basement is dark, except for a single dim lightbulb shining in the ceiling. There are cardboard boxes piled up high, and a tremendous amount of dust, just like StingRay said there would be. Lumphy can't see any ghosts or rats or axe murderers, but he is sure they are there, hiding in the corners, ready to pop out and scare a buffalo at any moment.

The Little Girl left him sitting in a laundry hamper. She's gone to ask for help with the soap. Next to the hamper, the Washing Machine looms, towering in all its metal whiteness and terrifying bigness. Lumphy shuts his eyes and tries not to ponder it.

But he ponders it anyway.

He could scramble out of the hamper, he thinks, and hide himself in a corner.

But no, there might be a ghost there.

And the Little Girl would miss him.

He could try to climb the stairs, but he is not sure he can make it. And even if he got to the top, the Girl would just find him on the floor and wash him anyway.

"I am a greasy buffalo," he says to himself, because it

sounds tough. But he doesn't feel much better, and shuts his eyes to block out the sight of the big Machine.

"Quiet, are you?" says a friendly voice. "Shoot. I was hoping for some company."

Lumphy opens one eye. "Who's talking?"

"Me, Frank," says the voice. "Who else would it be?"

"Frank?"

"The washer," says the Washing Machine.

Lumphy opens his other eye. The Machine isn't moving, but it is certainly making conversation. "I didn't expect you to talk," says Lumphy in a small voice.

"No one ever does. It's a lonely life," says Frank. "Just me and a dryer that never has anything interesting to say."

"Hmmmp," rumbles the Dryer, a large brown contraption sitting next to Frank.

"Well, you don't, do you?" says Frank testily.

"Ummmph," says the Dryer.

"This is how it is, all day," complains Frank. "She's never any fun. What's that on you—applesauce?"

"Peanut butter."

"Don't worry, I can fix you right up. Peanut butter is no problem. Done it tons of times before."

"It's very greasy."

"I'm an excellent washing machine. Top of my game, not that anyone really notices."

"TukTuk never told me about you," says Lumphy, standing up on his hind legs to peep over the edge of the laundry basket at Frank.

"What is TukTuk?"

"A towel. A yellow one, with frayed edges."

"I think I've seen her around."

"Ummmrgh," complains the Dryer.

"Exactly," says Frank. "Those towels are stuck-up. None of them ever says a word to either one of us. It's like they think they're so popular."

"Do you talk to *them*?" asks Lumphy.

"Oh, they're busy amongst themselves," says Frank. "I can't get a word in edgewise, not that they'd pay me any mind."

"TukTuk is beautiful," says Lumphy, who is very loyal.

"Pretty is as pretty does, that's what I say."

"Maybe she doesn't know you talk?"

Frank had never thought of that.

"If you don't talk to her, I bet she doesn't know," says Lumphy, feeling helpful.

· · · · ·

The Little Girl's father puts Lumphy into Frank's washtub, adds a sprinkling of powdered soap, and presses a button. Warm water pours in. The tub is rumbling.

"Frank!" yells Lumphy, anxious to be heard above the din. "I don't feel good. Will you stop, please?"

"Can't stop," says Frank importantly. "It's a cycle."

"I feel sick!"

"What a cycle means," explains Frank, "is that I have to see it through to the end."

"How long does it last?"

"Twenty-two minutes. Agitation, rinse, second rinse, and spin. You have nineteen minutes left."

"It's uncomfortable," moans Lumphy, as the water sloshes him back and forth.

"Think of it like a dance," says Frank. "Then maybe you won't feel sick."

"But there's no music."

So Frank begins to sing:

> "Shuffle-o
> Shuffle-o
> Greasy little
> Buffalo
> Tough-y little buffle-y
> Dance that buffalo shuffle with me!

Dance, dance, prance, prance

Dance that buffalo shuffle with me!"

Lumphy likes the idea of a buffalo shuffle. He does feel queasy during the agitation, but Frank keeps singing as Lumphy sloshes around, and by the first rinse cycle—when the clean, cool water pours in to wash the soap and peanut butter away—the buffalo is starting to enjoy himself. "Dance, dance, prance, prance!" he sings along with Frank, waggling his tail and clapping his front paws together.

By the second rinse he is kicking up his back legs and yelling "tough-y little buffle-y" as loud as he can yell. And when the spin cycle arrives, he forgets completely that spinning makes his stomach feel funny. "Wheeeee!" cries Lumphy. "Look at meeeeee!"

Then the wash is over. The Girl's father pulls him out to go hang on a clothesline in the open air.

"Goodbye, Frank!" Lumphy calls as the basement door shuts. "You have a wonderful singing voice."

"Thank you!" calls Frank. "It's nice to have someone appreciate it."

"Urrgmh," says the Dryer.

. . . . .

Lumphy goes on another picnic the next weekend. Same pond, same sandwiches. It doesn't look like rain, though, so his chances of going home in the picnic basket are slim.

When the Little Girl and her father are feeding the ducks, and Lumphy knows they aren't looking, he (very cleverly) unscrews the lid of the jam jar and dips his nose and forefeet into the apricot goo.

"I am a sticky buffalo," he says to himself. "And when I get home, I am going to visit Frank."

Sitting there in the sunshine on the picnic blanket, he begins to sing:

"Shuffle-o

Shuffle-o

Sticky little

Buffalo

Tough-y little buffle-y

Dance that buffalo shuffle with me!

Dance, dance, prance, prance

Dance that buffalo shuffle with me!"

CHAPTER FOUR

✢

The Possible Shark

Plastic is going to the beach. The Little Girl told her specially this morning, and she is excited—though not sure what to expect.

"Stingrays know all about the beach. Would you like me to tell you?" asks StingRay. She and Plastic are playing checkers.

Plastic says Yes.

"The main thing is bigness. The ocean goes on and on forever."

"Is there clover?" asks the one-eared sheep, who is watching the game with Lumphy.

"No clover," says StingRay, moving red.

"Grass?"

"No. It's the ocean."

"Oh, well." Sheep goes back to watching.

"Is it bigger than the pond?" asks Plastic, moving black across the board.

"A zillion times bigger," answers StingRay.

"I can't wait!" cries Plastic, and hums a happy hum. "Beach beach beach!"

For a second, StingRay is quiet. She is wondering why she isn't going to the beach with Plastic. Or even *instead* of Plastic—who after all has only lived with the Little Girl since last September. "You won't like it," StingRay says, finally, hopping red over one of Plastic's black checkers.

"Yes I will. Beach!" yells Plastic.

"No you won't," StingRay repeats. "The water goes down further than anybody can see. It's dangerous, if you're not a fish."

"I'm a great floater." Plastic pushes her black checker to the back of the board. "King me!"

"It doesn't matter," says StingRay. "The beach is only safe for stingrays,

and salmons,

and goldfish.

"There are dangers in the bigness that only fish like me know about," she continues.

"Jellyfish made of grape and raspberry jelly,

And octopi with eleven hundred legs,

And worst of all, garbage-eating sharks."

"What about the Little Girl?" Lumphy has stopped concentrating on the game.

"She'll be okay. She's a good swimmer," answers StingRay. "She's been to school."

"Beach beach beach!" yells Plastic. "King me!"

"If you're not going to listen, Plastic," says StingRay, "I don't know why you bothered asking. And," she adds, moving away from the checkerboard, "I don't feel like playing anymore."

"*I'm* listening," says Lumphy. "What did you do when you went to the beach and met the garbage-eating shark?"

"Ummm," says StingRay, looking carefully at a fancy blue pillow that has captured her attention.

"Huh?"

"Hrrmplle mmmunuh nnn." StingRay nibbles on a bit of pillow fringe.

"Hey, did you *really* see a shark?" asks Plastic, accusingly.

"Well . . . ," mutters StingRay, inspecting the opposite corner of the pillow with great interest. "I just know about them, okay?"

"Did you even really *go* to the beach?" Plastic bounces up and down.

StingRay crawls under the pillow so her friends can't see her face. "Well, not in person."

"Beach beach beach!" yells Plastic again, rolling around in circles. "Does anyone want to finish the checker game? I have a king!"

"Shut up, Plastic!" says StingRay loudly. "I hope you go to the beach and never come back."

. . . . .

A few minutes later, the Little Girl packs Plastic in a tote bag along with a cotton blanket, sun protection, and some sand toys. Off they go for the day, happy as can be.

Back in the bedroom, StingRay has crawled under the blue pillow and won't come out. "Why didn't the Little

Girl take *me* to the beach?" she moans. "I'm the one who sleeps on the high bed. I'm the one who's a fish."

"People like bounce at the beach," comforts Lumphy, sitting near the pillow. "Plastic is bouncier than you are."

"Bouncers and floaters," adds the one-eared sheep, nibbling the pillow fringe.

"What?" asks StingRay.

"Floaters. Toy boats, bath toys. Bath toys go to the beach all the time."

"Do you think the Girl likes floaters better than sinkers?" wonders StingRay.

"I'm just saying, she takes them to the beach."

"I'm a sinker," says Lumphy. "What about you, Sheep?"

"A sinker for sure," says the sheep. "All this wool, weighs me down."

"I'm a floater," says StingRay in a loud voice.

"Are you?" asks Lumphy. "Wow."

"I can float as well as Plastic, any day."

. . . . .

StingRay spends the next hour thinking very hard.

Truth is, she has never floated in her life. She has never even gotten wet.

But the Little Girl likes floaters.

And a fish is a fish, and a fish should swim.

What if the Little Girl sees Plastic floating and loves her better than me? she wonders. *What if she loves her better,*

> *and starts to sleep with her on the high bed with*
>
> *the fluffy pillows,*
>
> *and sends me to the dump,*
>
> *and says "StingRay who?" whenever anyone*
>
> *mentions me?*

It is a terrible bunch of thoughts.

When no one is looking, StingRay sneaks down the hall to the bathroom.

TukTuk is there, hanging on a rod.

"Hello," says StingRay as if nothing is out of the

ordinary. "Don't let me bother you. I'm just going to do my regular floating that I do."

"Your tag says 'dry clean only,' " remarks TukTuk.

"So?" says StingRay. She puts the plug in the bathtub, turns on the water, and gets in.

"So that means don't take a bath."

"I'm a fish," says StingRay. "I can float." She sits in the tub, feeling the wetness seep into her plush belly and flippers.

"No you can't."

"Can, too! Look at me!"

"Your tummy is still on the floor of the tub."

"Mind your own business," snaps StingRay. "I'm doing my floating."

The water is icy cold. StingRay tries to ignore it. She is waiting for her tummy to come off the floor of the tub. Waiting for proof she is a floater.

But her tummy stays right where it is.

The water goes over her gills, then over her back.

It goes over her eyes, and covers the tip of her tail.

. . . . .

Plastic rides in the trunk of the car, where it is very hot. Then the car stops, and she is lifted out. The air is fresh and salty.

The ocean really does go on and on forever. Plastic can hardly keep from wiggling, she is so excited.

The Little Girl and her parents get their beach blanket and cooler and umbrella set up. They have paperback novels and a portable radio, too. The mother wears a baseball cap and a black bikini. She forces the Little Girl to put on suntan lotion, and the Girl whines. The father runs down to the water and back, yelling about how cold it is. The Girl drinks apple juice from a cardboard box.

Then Plastic is tossed straight up in the air until she nearly touches the sun.

She is rolled through tunnels of damp sand and comes out the other end.

She is the center of a game called Keep Away.

She is perched on top of a large sand castle.

She is tossed onto the surface of the ocean, where she floats upon the waves.

And floats.

And floats.

For longer than she'd like, floating all by herself.

And then, she is eaten.

An animal with musky, wet fur takes Plastic in its jaws with a sudden snap. She can feel the sharp teeth and the floppy warm tongue. The creature makes soft grunting noises as it paddles out of the ocean and onto the sand. Plastic tries to wiggle free, but it has her tight.

Is it a shark? Plastic wonders.

Does it think I'm a tasty piece of garbage?

The possible shark trots across the sand wagging its

tail. It heads a long way down the beach. Again, Plastic tries to get out of its grip, but it has a good hold. It trots and trots, occasionally poking her with its tongue.

Then the possible shark drops Plastic onto a pile of seaweed, pins her down with one enormous paw, and begins to chew.

. . . . .

In the tub, StingRay is completely underwater.

At the beach, a possible-shark tooth pops Plastic's rubber skin.

In the tub, StingRay is soaked through her sawdust insides.

At the beach, the air whizzes out of Plastic until she is soft and squashy.

StingRay tries to lift a flipper to pull herself out, but the water makes her so heavy she can't move.

The possible shark tries to swallow Plastic.

StingRay: "Help!"

Plastic: "Stop!"

Help!

Stop!

But TukTuk can't move, and the possible shark isn't listening.

. . . . .

Plastic is stuck in the back of the possible shark's throat. Very uncomfortable.

"Gagaglah." The possible shark chokes, coughs, chokes again, coughs—and spits Plastic out onto a pile of seaweed.

Plastic knows she has to get away fast. But what can she do? She is halfway deflated, very un-bouncy. The possible shark licks its chops—but as it swoops in for another chomp, Plastic turns her body so her puncture hole is pointing right at its face. Then she squeezes her rubbery skin together as tight as it will go, pushing her last bit of air out the puncture with a loud, farty noise.

PBBBLEH!

The possible shark is confused.

It pulls back.

It makes a whimpering sound.

Then it trots away, with its tail between its legs.

Yippee! thinks Plastic.

I can't stay here, though. It might come back, and eat me later.

The seaweed around her is gray-green and scraggly. There are clumps of it all over the beach, drifting in and out as the waves skim across the sand. Plastic checks to be sure no one is looking at her, then slips under a big piece. Rolling is hard with so little air inside, but she uses all her strength—and moves gently forward, and around, until she is wrapped thoroughly in seaweed. Then she waits until she hears a big wave crash on the shore.

As the ocean water rushes toward her, Plastic rolls along the edge of the water, pretending that the wave has caught this unsuspecting and surprisingly round blob of seaweed, and merely happens to be pulling it along. With each crash of the breakers, Plastic rolls a bit further in the direction of the Little Girl and her family.

Once, a wave really does catch her and she bangs up hard against a big rock.

Once, a small crab waves a mean-looking claw in her direction.

And once, a possible shark of a different nature (short legs, curly fur) sniffs her with frightening curiosity.

With tremendous effort, Plastic keeps moving until she hears the Little Girl's voice. Then she slips out of her seaweed cover and bold-face rolls back to the beach blanket, as fast as she can possibly roll.

. . . . .

StingRay is soaked through with cold water, and so heavy she cannot move. From the bottom of the tub, she hears a sound.

"Warble glub lub mangle."

Fortunately, her eyes are on the top of her head, so she can see what's above her. Lumphy and the one-eared sheep are sitting on the edge of the tub!

The rushing sound of the tap makes it impossible to make out what they are saying. And though she is glad to see them, StingRay can't think how they will rescue her, since both of them are sinkers.

After hating her friend all day, she wishes Plastic were here.

I was mean to her, thinks StingRay, *and now she's gone to the beach and might not ever return.*

I'm a sinker,

> *and a stinker, too,*

> *and if I rot and drown and dissolve in this tub,*

> *it is probably better than I deserve.*

"Warble glub lub mangle," StingRay hears again, and then—silence. Lumphy has turned off the tap.

"Glurb lurb swubbble wubble."

He has pulled up the plug by its chain, and the water is running out.

StingRay is humiliated. She almost wishes they hadn't found her, it is so embarrassing to be a soggy plush sinker fish.

And yet, she is very glad they did.

When the tub is empty, Lumphy and Sheep jump in and pull StingRay out. She is soaked through. They yank TukTuk down from the rod and wrap StingRay in the towel; then Lumphy jumps up and down on both of them to squeeze out as much of the water as possible. Then he and Sheep hang TukTuk back up and help StingRay to a nice sunny spot by the window in the bedroom, where she can dry herself the rest of the way.

StingRay can barely mutter "Thank you"—but Lumphy and Sheep don't mind.

. . . . .

The Little Girl's mommy has industrial-strength tape and a bicycle pump. When the family gets home from the beach, she brings Plastic down to the basement, tapes her puncture shut, and pumps her full of air.

Plastic is carried upstairs to the bedroom good as new, except for the small patch of clear tape covering the hole. She can sense it whenever she rolls—a slightly lumpy feeling—but she hopes no one else will notice.

It is excellent to have her bounce back.

It will be excellent to see Lumphy.

It will be excellent to see the sheep.

It will even be excellent to see StingRay, in spite of the mean thing she said about hoping Plastic went to the beach and never came back.

As soon as the Girl's mommy puts her on the bedroom rug and heads back downstairs, Plastic starts singing a song she made up in the car on the way home:

"I'm a small ball, small ball, small ball!

Not a snowball, snowball, snowball!

Not a meatball, meatball, meatball!

Not an eyeball, eyeball, eyeball!"

But she stops after a while, because nobody is listening. Lumphy, Sheep, and the toy mice are all clustered around the rocking horse in the corner, discussing whether or not it would be safe to try to use a hair dryer on StingRay.

"Lumphy!" cries Plastic. "Beach, beach, beach!"

"How was it?" Lumphy turns around.

"Yippee!" cries Plastic. "I floated and floated."

"Did you see fish?"

"Sharks!" says Plastic. "With big long legs and waggly tails. They were running all over."

"Wow." Lumphy is impressed. "Did the ocean go on forever?"

"Forever and ever."

"Was it much bigger than the pond?"

"A zillion times bigger."

Then Plastic spots StingRay, all damp on the window-sill. "What happened?" she whispers. "She's so soggy!"

Lumphy explains about the tub.

"Poor StingRay!" Plastic remembers how it felt without her bounce—how she could hardly roll, and how she doesn't want anyone to know. She thinks about how Lumphy is not quite a real buffalo, and StingRay is not quite a real stingray—but how she is a real ball, and can do all the stuff that balls can do.

She feels lucky.

"Did you know there is more than one kind of stingray?" wonders Plastic in a loud voice, loud enough for StingRay to hear all the way over by the window. "I read it in the animal book," she lies. "There are water stingrays and dry-clean-only stingrays. Dry-clean-only ones are bigger and stronger and much better-looking. And they live on land, and other animals look up to them because they know a lot of stuff. Which kind is our StingRay, I wonder?"

"Dry clean only," says StingRay in a small voice from the windowsill, feeling a tiny bit proud for the first time in a good while. "It says so on my tag."

"I thought so," says Plastic. "Because you're awfully big and you know so much."

There is a pause. "It's nice to have you home," says StingRay.

"Really?" asks Plastic.

"Yes," says StingRay. "It was very un-bouncy around here without you."

CHAPTER FIVE

✦

How Lumphy Got on the Big High Bed and Lost Something Rather Good-Looking

Every night, StingRay goes up on the big high bed to sleep. Lumphy, Plastic, the one-eared sheep, and the toy mice all stay on the floor.

The bed is a nice place to be. It has a warm patchwork quilt and four fluffy pillows. On the table next to it stand a glass of water and a stack of books.

Every night, StingRay gets to cuddle with the Little Girl. StingRay even goes under the covers.

Lumphy has only been on the bed for short visits, and Plastic has never been up there at all.

"Why you, every single night?" asks Lumphy, when StingRay comes down one morning to play on the shaggy rug where he, Sheep, and Plastic are sitting around doing nothing. "Why not me?"

"You have to be clean to go in the bed," says StingRay. "There can't be crumbs and peanut butter up there."

"Why not Plastic, then?"

"You have to be furry," says StingRay. "Balls don't ever go."

"It used to be *me*, before she came," mutters Sheep.

"I don't care," chirps Plastic, who has been spending much of her nights rolling down the stairs and then bouncing back up again three at a time. "Do you want to come watch me on the steps, Lumphy? I roll down like a race car!"

"Not really," says Lumphy. "I've seen you roll before."

"It's totally different on the *stairs*," pleads Plastic.

"It doesn't seem fair," says Lumphy to StingRay, "that you go up on the high bed every single night. What do you *do* up there?"

"Private stuff," says StingRay. "Between me and the Little Girl."

"But why don't I get to do private stuff?"

"Sorry. It's not like I have a choice. The Little Girl takes me. She wants me, I guess, because of how much she loves me."

"She loves me, too," says Lumphy.

"Of course she does. Just not enough to go up on the high bed. Don't feel bad."

"Hrrummmph." Lumphy turns his tail to StingRay and pretends to be interested in a bit of orange fluff he sees on the rug.

"Lumphy?"

Lumphy nuzzles the bit of fluff and doesn't answer.

"Want to go look out the window?"

Lumphy mumbles quietly to the bit of fluff as if he doesn't hear.

"Or watch television?"

He doesn't answer.

"We could play marbles."

The fluff is taking all Lumphy's attention. It takes up all his attention for the entire day. He won't talk to StingRay at all.

. . . . .

The next morning Lumphy starts looking at the fluff again as soon as StingRay comes down from the bed. He looks at it all morning, all afternoon, and all evening.

He does this for six days.

On the seventh day, StingRay comes down and pokes him in the shoulder. "Know what?" she says. "I have an idea for getting the Girl to bring you up on the bed. Do you want to hear it?"

Lumphy stops looking at the fluff and looks at StingRay instead.

"We can decorate you," she says. "To make you more of a bedtime buffalo. We could drape you in rabbit fur and flannel,

and put a big pair of fuzzy slippers

on your feet,

and maybe some bows and ribbons

on your tail,

and some pink and yellow feathers.

You will look so cuddly, she will have to take

you to bed."

"Hrmmh," says Lumphy.

"What?"

"Is there another option?"

"Sure. We could break your tail.

　　Just a small break near the end,

　　maybe by using a hammer on it when nobody

　　is looking,

　　and then you would be injured.

　　The Little Girl would wrap your bottom up

　　in toilet paper and masking tape,

　　and bring you to the bed to get well."

"What if *you* pretend to be lost in the closet?" suggests Lumphy. "Then she'd take me, I bet."

StingRay doesn't think that would work.

"I read something you could try," pipes up Plastic, who has been listening in from a spot underneath the bed. "But it's not very nice."

"What?" Lumphy wants to know.

"It's a trick. They used it in old TV commercials and science experiments. Sub-lim-in-al messages."

"Oooooh! Submarine messages!" cries StingRay. "Why didn't I think of them before?"

"What are they?" asks Lumphy.

"Uhhh . . . It's too complicated to explain," stalls StingRay. "Isn't it, Plastic?"

Plastic pauses. "I can explain a little bit," she finally says.

"Oh, a little bit, sure. That we could do," says StingRay. "You go ahead."

"I read that in supermarkets they used to have secret messages playing very quietly under the music that people didn't know their brains could hear," begins Plastic. "Messages that would say, 'Buy sugar cereal,' or 'You need to eat a lot of meat, buy it here.' The messages would get the shoppers to do what they said."

"This isn't a supermarket," says Lumphy.

"Duh," says Plastic. "But we could do like this:

StingRay could whisper in the Little Girl's ear while she's asleep. When the Girl wakes up, she'll think whatever StingRay has told her."

"Oooooh." StingRay is silent for a moment. "What if I whisper, 'Don't eat your vegetables'?

or 'Sit in front of the TV all day like a giant

wet noodle'?

or 'Cheat at card games'?

What if my submarine message is

'Buy StingRay lots of presents'?

Will she really do whatever I say?" StingRay

feels a thrill.

Plastic rolls side to side, nervously. "Forget I told you about it. It only maybe works, anyway."

"If it maybe works, I want to try it," insists Lumphy.

"I shouldn't have mentioned it," says Plastic. "It's a bad idea."

"Then how am I going to get on the bed?" cries

Lumphy, looking up at the fluffy pillows from his spot on the rug. "I have to get up there!"

"Don't worry," says StingRay. "I've done submarine messages lots of times before. I'll get you up."

It is hard to think about sharing the big high bed—in fact, StingRay doesn't want to share it at all. But even more, she doesn't want Lumphy to ignore her and stare at his bit of fluff all day. That evening, StingRay stays awake when the Little Girl falls asleep.

"Bring Lumphy to bed,
Bring Lumphy to bed,
Bring Lumphy to bed,
Bring Lumphy to bed,"
she whispers long into the night.

· · · · ·

The next evening, after brushing her teeth and putting on her pajamas, the Little Girl lifts Lumphy up along with StingRay. The submarine message has worked!

Lumphy is so excited. Cool white pillows, patchwork quilt, warm flannel sheets, private time! He can hardly believe it's true.

But here is what happens, up on the high bed:

Not much. The Girl's father reads three stories aloud. He sings a short lullaby. The Girl kisses her father four times. He turns out the light and leaves.

Then the Girl kisses StingRay and Lumphy, tucks them under the covers, and goes right to sleep.

StingRay goes to sleep, too.

Lumphy lies there and stares at the ceiling.

He stares at the clock, which glows in the dark.

He stares at the curtains, blowing slightly in the wind.

He doesn't feel sleepy.

"Psst. StingRay," he whispers.

StingRay doesn't answer.

"StingRay!" he whispers again, nipping her gently on the cheek.

"What?" StingRay sounds muddled.

"Want to play I Spy?"

"It's dark. I can't spy anything."

"I need a drink of water," moans Lumphy.

"No you don't."

"Then I need another story. Will you tell me a story?"

"I can't think of one now," says StingRay. "I'm trying to sleep."

"Want to sing 'Camptown Races'?"

"No."

"Just a little bit? I think it will help me relax. Camptown Racetrack sing a song . . ."

"Doo dah, doo dah," mumbles StingRay softly, and closes her eyes.

Lumphy stares at the ceiling again.

He stares at the clock.

He stares at the curtains.

He still doesn't feel sleepy. He crawls to the edge of the high bed and looks down.

The toy mice are playing leapfrog. Plastic is reading one of the big books and rolling slightly side to side. The one-eared sheep is laughing with the wooden rocking horse in the corner.

Lumphy sighs, and rearranges himself on the bed. The problem is, he usually stays up late. This time of night, he likes to be doing stuff. Playing marbles, or checkers, or pick-up sticks. Something.

It is not his bedtime yet. Not even close.

Bonk! Lumphy jumps down. It hurts his bottom when he lands, but he doesn't mind. He is so happy to be down again that he kisses all four toy mice with his buffalo mouth and then trots over to Plastic and offers to watch her roll down the staircase.

. . . . .

Every night after that, the Little Girl takes Lumphy to bed with her. Lumphy feels he's got it made—all the importance and extra kisses of going to sleep on the high bed, and none of the boringness. He just waits until the Girl is asleep, then hops down—Bonk!—and lives it up until midnight, when he (very cleverly) positions himself below the edge of the bed, so it looks like he fell off by mistake, and goes to sleep till morning.

StingRay feels this behavior is disrespectful. "It's an honor to sleep on the high bed," she complains. "You're not taking it seriously."

She, Lumphy, and Plastic are watching cartoons in the living room while the Little Girl is at school. "I'm not sleepy at eight," Lumphy says, when the show goes to a commercial.

"Fine, then," says StingRay. "Don't get up on the bed."

"It's not like I have a choice now." Lumphy is smug.

"The Little Girl takes me. She wants me, I guess, because of how much she loves me."

"When it's bedtime," explains StingRay, "you're supposed to get in bed and stay there until morning."

"Why?"

"Because people bigger than you want you to," pipes up Plastic. "That's why."

"Who knows the difference?" Lumphy asks. "The Little Girl doesn't know I'm hopping down."

"*I* know," says StingRay. "And I don't like it."

"What *she* doesn't know won't hurt her. And I'm not sleepy at eight." Lumphy goes back to watching the cartoon.

. . . . .

But the Little Girl is no dummy. She notices Lumphy on the floor each morning by the side of the bed. One night, she gets a length of shiny green ribbon and ties it to his tail. She ties the other end to her bedpost. "You won't fall out now, sweetie buffalo," she says, kissing his head an extra time to make up for all the bumps he must have suffered in his falls.

"StingRay, look at my tail!" whispers Lumphy, when the lights are out and the Girl is asleep. "Take the ribbon off!"

"No."

"Why not?"

"The Girl wants you to have that ribbon. She goes to school. She knows what's best for you."

"I know what's best for me," says Lumphy. "And this ribbon is not it."

StingRay wrinkles her nose. "You got covered with peanut butter, and then you got covered with jam,

and then cookie batter,

and hummus,

and soy sauce.

You're always getting dirty. How is that someone who knows what's best?"

"I'm older now," says Lumphy. He walks to the edge of the bed, stretching the ribbon tightly. He leans forward, and feels the pull on his tail. "StingRay, help me!" he cries. "I'm tied up like a balloon!"

"You wouldn't be, if you'd stayed where you belong."

"My tail is killing me!" says Lumphy, lying. "I need to get down!"

"Be quiet, or you'll wake the Little Girl." StingRay flips over and closes her eyes.

. . . . .

Being tied up makes Lumphy feel frantic. The knots in the ribbon get tighter and tighter the more he pulls. He tugs harder and harder, grunting his buffalo grunts, and finally jumps off the edge of the bed with the ribbon still attached to his tail.

There is no bonk. Lumphy is upside down, tail side up, hanging in the air. He feels sick to his stomach.

He tries to scramble back up the side of the bed, but he can't get his feet turned around the right way.

He wiggles and tries to lift his head up to chew on the ribbon, but his body is not very flexible.

He is stuck.

"Lumphy!" It is Plastic, rolling across the rug toward him. "Why are you upside down?"

"Untie me," cries Lumphy.

"No hands," says Plastic.

"Pull me."

"No arms."

"Chew through the ribbon."

"No teeth," says Plastic. "It's normal for a ball."

"What *can* you do?"

"Bounce."

"Bounce me, then," says Lumphy. "Please."

Plastic rolls back to get a good start, and then she bounces herself hard at Lumphy, banging him against the side of the bed.

"Harder!" cries Lumphy.

Plastic bounces harder.

And again.

And a really hard bounce.

There is a ripping sound. "You're breaking the ribbon!" cries Lumphy. "Keep going!"

Plastic does. Another ripping sound.

"Again, again! I'm almost down!"

One more bounce, and Lumphy crashes to the ground. Bonk!

He lands on his bottom, just like before. Only it feels diffcrent.

It feels like something is missing.

Something is.

Lumphy looks up at the unbroken ribbon, dangling from the top of the high bed. Something short and chocolate brown and rather good-looking is attached to it.

"Is that my tail?" cries Lumphy.

"Ummm," says Plastic. "It probably might be."

"I need it! I need it!" Lumphy is in tears.

"There, there."

"What will I do without it?"

"There, there."

"Oh, I need it very badly!"

"What for?" Plastic wants to know.

Lumphy sniffs back his tears. He tries to think of an answer.

"You look tougher without it," says Plastic kindly, rolling around to examine Lumphy's bottom.

"Really?"

"None of the tough buffaloes have tails," lies Plastic. "I read it in the animal book."

"They don't?"

"It's the tough-buffalo fashion."

Lumphy thinks for a minute. "Who needs a tail, anyway?" he sniffs.

"I don't," says Plastic.

"I don't, either, then," says Lumphy, bravely.

· · · · ·

About an hour later, while Lumphy is showing his tail stump to TukTuk in the bathroom, Plastic hears a noise from on top of the high bed.

It sounds like whispering.

It sounds like StingRay.

It sounds an awful lot like a submarine message. "Lumphy murrphle wuffle rmmm floor murrphle. Lumphy murrphle wuffle rmmm floor murrphle."

· · · · ·

The next day, the Little Girl wraps Lumphy's bottom in toilet paper and masking tape to help it feel better. But she does not take him to bed with her that night.

In fact, she never takes him to bed again.

Lumphy doesn't mind, though. He is leapfrogging, and laughing, and listening to TukTuk explain about hand lotion and dental floss.

He is staying up late.

After all, he's not sleepy at eight.

CHAPTER SIX

❖

It Is Difficult to Find
the Right Birthday Present

The Little Girl's birthday is in a week. She will be seven. There are big plans. A party, a cake, a piñata. Friends are coming over.

"Seven is old," muses Plastic, as she and StingRay look out the window one day while the Girl is at school. "Will she be a grown-up soon?"

"No," says StingRay.

"How can you tell?"

"You're not a grown-up until you're at least eight." StingRay taps the windowpane with her flipper for emphasis.

"How old are *you*?" Plastic wants to know.

"When you're eight, you can drive a limousine," StingRay explains,

> "and you brush your teeth without being
>
> reminded,
>
> and you can read all the words in the
>
> dictionary, no matter how long.
>
> You have lots of money to buy all the
>
> chocolate you want,
>
> and poofy dresses and cool soccer shoes,
>
> plus anything blue that strikes your fancy.
>
> But not when you're seven."

"How old are *you*?" asks Plastic again.

"That doesn't matter," says StingRay. "What matters is how much stuff I know. People who know a lot of stuff don't need birthdays."

. . . . .

"I'm having a party for my toys," the Little Girl tells her three best friends. "In the morning, before the kids come over. With my tea set and a real cupcake. Everybody is invited."

They begin whispering as soon as the Girl leaves for school. "Who's included in *Everybody*?" Lumphy wonders.

"Just everybody," says Plastic.

"Does it mean me?"

"Of course."

"Does it mean the toy mice?"

"I think so."

"What about the rocking horse? He can't sit at the table."

"Oh, um . . ." Plastic rolls side to side a bit, not answering.

"*Everybody* is us three, the toy mice, and the one-eared sheep," explains StingRay. "That's who's invited."

"That's all?" says Lumphy. "I feel bad about the horse."

"Well, maybe the horse can come," says StingRay. "We could have the party over in his corner."

"What about Frank?" wonders Lumphy. "What about TukTuk?"

"Frank has to stay in the basement," StingRay points out.

"TukTuk probably wouldn't even *want* to come," says Plastic. "It's not a towel kind of thing. She likes to do stuff with the other towels."

"I think she'd want to," says Lumphy. "She's the Little Girl's towel."

"If you invite one towel, you have to invite them all," StingRay explains. "The Girl has to keep the party down to a manageable size."

. . . . .

"What are you giving her?" Frank asks Lumphy, one afternoon when the buffalo is having maple syrup washed off in the basement.

"Giving who?" asks Lumphy.

"The Girl. You should give the Girl a present if you're going to her birthday party."

"I don't think she expects one."

"You have to get her something," says Frank. "It's manners."

Lumphy is worried now. "What can I get?"

"Well, what does she love most?"

"I don't know!" cries Lumphy.

"Rrgaaaaah," says the Dryer, interrupting.

"She wishes she could go to the party," explains Frank. "We never go anywhere." He drains out his water tank and starts the spin cycle. "It's the loneliest life."

"Mrrrmmmnnnnh," says the Dryer soothingly. "Mrrmnnaaaaaah."

"True," says Frank. "We have each other."

. . . . .

As soon as he is clean and dry, Lumphy calls Plastic and StingRay to a meeting on the windowsill. "We have to give her a present," he announces. "It's manners for birthday parties."

"Ooooh!" cries StingRay. "I know! Let's give her an airplane,

and a ball gown,

and a big-screen, flat-screen, giant jumbo television,

and some gummy bears.

She'll be so surprised."

"Great," says Plastic. "Now, where do we get an airplane?"

"I know where. Don't worry about that," says StingRay. "How much money do we have?"

Plastic thinks for a moment. "We don't have any. Let's get the ball gown instead. Or do we need money for that, too?"

"We need money for *everything*," answers Lumphy.

"You're right!" cries Plastic in distress. "And even if we did have money, we can't get to the store because we're not eight yet, and we can't drive!"

"What does she love most?" asks Lumphy. "That's what we should get her."

"New plan!" announces StingRay. "We're finding a present in the house."

. . . . .

The night before the birthday, StingRay only pretends to go to sleep with the Little Girl. Really, she flops down onto the shaggy rug and organizes a serious present hunt. "Don't come back without a quality gift!" she commands Plastic and Lumphy, standing on her tail and flapping her flippers.

Plastic is assigned to search the living room. It's mainly grown-up stuff, but she finds some books that look interesting, and a potted marigold. She can't move them, though, without arms or legs. She bounces back upstairs and asks the toy mice to help her. They do, but they're quite crabby about it. They insist that their names go on the card if the books or the marigold get chosen to be the present.

Lumphy is in charge of the basement. There's not a lot down there. He finds a can of creamed corn among the cardboard boxes, and carries it upstairs in his mouth. His jaw feels stiff by the time he gets back to the bedroom.

StingRay searches the closets. She almost gets squashed when a pile of sweaters falls on her head, and she bangs her flipper in a door, but she comes up with a blue T-shirt, a purse with snaps on it, and a hairbrush.

When the items are piled in the center of the shaggy rug, the toys sit all three together, thinking. "The best present is what she would love most," says Lumphy. "Is there anything here?"

"She likes blue," says StingRay. "The blue T-shirt is good."

"I think it's you that likes blue," says Plastic, with a gentle cough.

"Everyone likes blue," says StingRay. "It's the best color."

"But she already owns that shirt," says Plastic. "She wore it yesterday."

"She owns the books, too," points out Lumphy. "And the purse. And the marigold."

"And the hairbrush. And the corn!" moans Plastic.

"This is terrible!" cries StingRay. "Why didn't I think of this? She's going to be angry. She's going to cry because she's got no present,

and she'll throw the pillows at us,

and call us names,

and never invite us to any

of her parties again,

all because we couldn't find what she

would love most,

or even a second-rate present

on her birthday."

"I don't know about that," says Plastic.

"Why not?"

"Because we're her best friends. She said so at show-and-tell."

"So?"

"She wouldn't throw pillows at her best friends."

"If we're her best friends," says Lumphy, sadly, "we should know what she would love most."

"You're right," says Plastic. "We should."

But Plastic doesn't know.

And StingRay doesn't, either.

They sit there in silence for seven minutes and twenty-two seconds. Then, in a flash, Lumphy thinks he knows. His idea is such a good one that he waggles his tail stump with excitement and claps his buffalo forefeet together before scampering off in search of wrapping paper.

. . . . .

On the morning of her birthday, the Little Girl wakes up to find two funny-shaped packages, and one perfectly round package, sitting on the windowsill of her room. Two are tied up with green ribbon, and one is tied up with blue. Neither of the grown-ups is awake yet. The

Girl gets up in bare feet. "Presents!" she cries, scooping all three into her arms and setting them on the bed.

She unwraps the small, round one first. "What a beautiful, fat ball you are!" she says, hugging Plastic to her chest. Plastic wants to bounce, she is so happy, but she keeps still so the Girl won't see how excited she is.

The bumpy package is next. "Oh, it's you, you sweetie, sweetie buffalo!" cries the Girl as Lumphy comes out of the tissue paper. Lumphy doesn't mind the sweetie sweetie thing, even though he is tough, because he gets several extra kisses.

Finally, the Little Girl unwraps the flat package. "You even used blue ribbon!" she laughs, squeezing StingRay hard. "My favorite!"

"I told you so," whispers StingRay from her position on the Girl's lap. "It's just the best color."

. . . . .

The birthday party is a great success. TukTuk is invited after all. In fact, she serves as a tablecloth!

The Girl has laid out her china tea set in front of the rocking horse in the corner. There is a nosegay of flowers, and she serves real chamomile tea. There are cups and saucers enough for everyone, even all the toy mice.

In front of the Girl is a special cupcake, decorated with white frosting and a blue rose. She cuts it with a butter knife. "Happy birthday, Lumphy!" she says, serving him a slice and a cup of tea. "You know, it's your birthday, too, today."

Lumphy is surprised, but he chuckles to himself.

"And happy birthday, Plastic!" says the Girl.

"Am I one already?" wonders Plastic.

StingRay looks up at the Girl, expecting to be next. But the Girl is busy. She's serving tea and cupcake to Sheep, Plastic, the rocking horse, TukTuk, and the toy

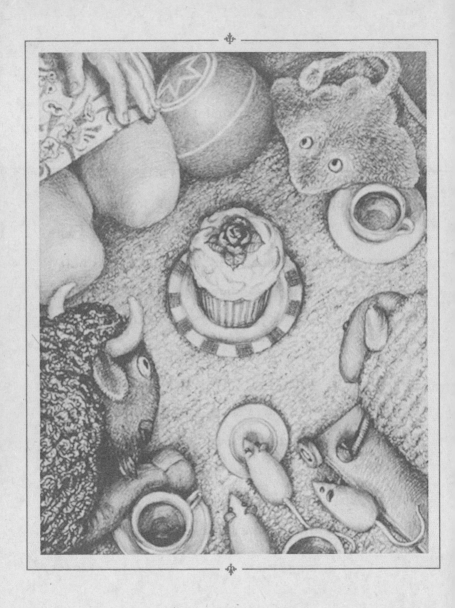

mice. "Three birthdays all on the same day?" whispers StingRay. "That doesn't seem right."

"Who cares?" says Plastic.

"I like having a birthday," says Lumphy.

"Is this banana cake?" Sheep sniffs at her piece.

Everyone has cake but StingRay. "I don't think the Girl knows what she's talking about," whispers StingRay. "That's all I'm saying."

"I think it might be vanilla," says Lumphy.

"Will there be seconds?" the sheep wonders aloud.

"It's not like I care," adds StingRay. "I don't need a birthday."

"And now," announces the Little Girl, "a very special happy birthday to my extra-best friend, *StingRay*!" She cuts off the piece of cupcake with the blue frosting rose on it, and serves it onto StingRay's plate. "Lumphy, I got you when I turned five. Then you, Plastic, when I turned six!

But I've had StingRay since I turned four." She reaches over and scratches where the ears would be, if StingRay had ears. "I hope you all have the best birthdays in the world."

"Ooohhh," cries StingRay, leaning into the scratch. "It's my birthday, too!"

"Happy birthday," says Lumphy.

"And she gave me the frosting rose."

" 'Cause it's your birthday!" cries Plastic.

"Yes, it is," says StingRay. "Didn't I tell you before?"

. . . . .

Late that night, when StingRay and the Little Girl are supposedly asleep in the big high bed, Plastic and Lumphy hear a song coming from up there.

"Sting-RAY, diddle-eye-oh,

Birth-DAY, diddle-eye-ee,

Who's got a birthday?

StingRay, StingRay!

Diddle-eye, Diddle-ee,

That means me!"

If Lumphy stands on tiptoe, he can see StingRay's flippers waving around in a dance.

Toy Dance Party

Being the further adventures of
a bossy-boots stingray, a courageous buffalo,
and a hopeful round someone called Plastic

"Makes ideal bedtime reading, preferably aloud." —*The Wall Street Journal*

Toy Dance Party

by Emily Jenkins ✦ pictures by Paul O. Zelinsky

by Emily Jenkins
Illustrated by Paul O. Zelinsky

CHAPTER ONE

❦

The Toys Are Left In

Lumphy, the stuffed buffalo, did not go with the Girl on winter vacation.

StingRay did not go, either. She thought she would. The Girl even told her she would, because she and StingRay sleep together, every single night, on the high bed with the fluffy pillows. But in the end, when the suitcases were packed and the car loaded, the Girl and her parents drove away—and StingRay was left behind.

Plastic, being only a ball, had not expected to go on the trip. No one plays with balls in snowy weather. She is here with StingRay and Lumphy in the empty house, finding it strange to have days go by without the good-natured ruckus of the people who live there. No alarm clocks, no morning bustle, no baths, no cooking smells. No laughter, no arguments, no stories read aloud.

The house is cold.

For several days—they are not sure how many—Lumphy, StingRay, and Plastic play checkers and Hungry Hungry Hippos with the toy mice and the one-eared sheep. They chat with the rocking horse in the corner and with TukTuk, the old yellow towel in the hallway bathroom. They watch television. But the hours go by much more slowly than usual. There is always the feeling of someone missing. The Girl they love.

"When is she coming back, again?" Plastic wonders one afternoon. She and Lumphy are on the windowsill, downstairs in the living room. Lumphy is watching the

snow falling outside, and Plastic has been reading a book about cheese—kinds of cheese, where it comes from, and how it's made. She is flipping the pages herself with a rolling technique she's invented.

"The Saturday before school starts again, is what they said," Lumphy answers. He feels sick to his stomach when he thinks about how the Girl isn't here.

"What Saturday is that?" Plastic asks.

"I don't know. A week is how long they'll be gone."

"But how long is a week?" Plastic persists.

"StingRay says five days."

"What day is it now?" wonders Plastic. "Is it Tuesday? I think it's maybe Tuesday." She rocks anxiously from side to side.

"Urmph," mumbles Lumphy. He is counting in his head.

"What are the days besides Tuesday, anyhow?" continues Plastic. "Does it go Onesday, Tuesday, Threesday, Foursday?"

"I think they have already been gone *more* than five days," announces Lumphy.

"You mean we already had Tuesday?"

"I mean we already had *Saturday*," says Lumphy. "I mean, the week is up."

Fwap! Gobble-a gobble-a.

Fwap! Gobble-a gobble-a.

They are interrupted.

Fwap! Gobble-a gobble-a.

StingRay is falling down the stairs. Flipper over plush flipper, bouncing first off the wall, then off the posts beneath the banister.

Fwap! Gobble-a gobble-a.

Fwap! Gobble-a gobble-a. And then eventually: Bonk! She lands at the bottom.

Lumphy climbs gingerly off the windowsill while Plastic bounces over to StingRay. "Are you okay?"

StingRay is lying on her back, and her head hurts where she banged it on a post, but she quickly turns over on her tummy and brushes her eye with her left flipper. "What do you mean?"

"You fell down the stairs."

"I don't know what you're talking about. I come down that way all the time on purpose." StingRay changes the subject. "What have you been doing?"

"I was reading!" Plastic tells her. "Did you know cheese is made in caves? Because it is! You put milk in a cave and out comes cheese!"

"Of course I knew that," says StingRay, although she didn't. "Listen. Do you know where the playing cards are? I can't find them anywhere and I want to play Fish."

Plastic and Lumphy agree to help look for the cards. They search the downstairs, checking bookshelves and the drawers of the coffee table—but the cards are not there. They go upstairs: Lumphy climbing, StingRay lurching up each step with a strong push of her tail, and Plastic bouncing easily, five stairs at a time.

They look through the Girl's bedroom again. Search

under the high bed. Look behind the box that holds the board games.

Then they realize: the Girl has packed the cards. She has taken them with her on vacation, where she has not taken Lumphy, or Plastic, or StingRay.

"What else has she packed?" cries StingRay, frantic. She flops herself across the bedroom carpet. "Did she pack that book about the mouse in the dungeon?"

Plastic takes a high bounce to look on the bedside table. "It's not here."

"Now we'll never find out what happens!" moans StingRay. "What else did she pack?"

Their survey reveals that the Girl has packed not only the book about the mouse in the dungeon *and* the deck of cards but

a box of dominoes,

a carton of LEGOs,

a paint box and a pad of art paper,

a jigsaw puzzle of a triceratops,

two Barbie dolls that don't talk and

never have,

and a vinyl box of Barbie outfits.

"Oh no!" StingRay cries when Plastic and Lumphy present her with the total. "Why did she take all the second-rate toys and leave us?"

"There, there," says Plastic. "She just . . ."

"She just what? She just forgot us, that's what! Forgot us and took those Barbie dolls who don't even say anything at all!"

"Maybe she went to a place that was good for Barbies," says Plastic. "Some kind of special Barbie place, where stingrays would get bored."

"Oh yeah?" StingRay throws herself on the carpet in distress. "And she needs her paint box there?

And her *dominoes*?

She hardly even likes the dominoes.

She never does puzzles!

She doesn't love me!

She's left me!"

"She's coming back," says Plastic. "She's coming back on Saturday." She doesn't tell StingRay what Lumphy told her—that maybe Saturday is already over.

"By Saturday she'll have forgotten all about us!" cries StingRay. Now she is twisting over and back on the carpet, gasping and sobbing.

And sobbing some more.

And even more sobbing.

This can't go on, thinks Lumphy. He has to do something.

He galumphs down the hall to the bathroom and grabs TukTuk, the faded yellow towel that hangs over the rack. Holding her corner in his mouth, he drags her as fast as he can into the Girl's bedroom, where StingRay is tossing and flopping. With one big motion, Lumphy throws TukTuk on top of StingRay, covering her eyes, her flippers, her whole body.

"Where are the lights?" StingRay yells.

It's all yellow in here!

I'm going blind.

I'll never see another sunrise.

Lumphy will have to lead me around

so I don't bump into furniture!"

StingRay is still twisting and crying, but the weight of TukTuk is such that she can no longer flip over. Lumphy backs up a couple of feet, and—rumpa lumpa, rumpa lumpa—jumps heavily onto TukTuk.

"Oh, umph!" cries StingRay. "You're on me, someone.

Someone's on me!

Someone heavy!

Oh heavens!

I knew it would come to this, some horrible day.

No one loves me!

I'm being squished!

I'm blind and my friends are squishing me!"

Lumphy sits. He sits on TukTuk, who lies on StingRay, and together they calm her down, resting on her so she feels their weight.

The sobbing stops.

She is barely moving now. One flipper is just thumping up and down.

Finally, StingRay is peaceful.

Lumphy climbs down from her broad plush back and pulls TukTuk behind him. "The Girl still loves us," he says.

"Okay," says StingRay meekly. "I just got concerned for a minute."

· · · · ·

Half an hour later, all three toys are sitting on the windowsill in the living room. The snow is still coming down. Plastic is reading about cheese some more. StingRay is drawing shapes in the frost on the window-pane. And Lumphy is worrying.

"The Girl hasn't been here for a really, really long time," he says, breaking the silence.

"Where is she, again?" asks Plastic.

"Bolling. They said they were going to Bolling to see the grandpa."

"But where is Bolling?"

Lumphy does not answer.

"And *what* is Bolling?" wonders Plastic. "Is it a town, a hotel, a magical land, or what?"

Lumphy doesn't answer, because he doesn't know. "It has been more than five days," he says. "In fact, it has been *way* more than five days, and when it is more days than it is supposed to be, that means maybe the people are lost."

"Oh oh oh!" cries StingRay, suddenly afraid. "She loves us but she's lost!"

"Maybe everything is fine," Plastic says. "The Girl is just having fun in Bolling."

"We can *not* panic." Lumphy looks pointedly at

StingRay. "And we cannot pretend anymore." Looking now at Plastic: "I think something has gone wrong. I think the Girl is lost."

StingRay tries not to panic and makes a small noise like this: Frrrrrr, frrrrrr.

"I have to go outside and look for her," announces Lumphy. "The Girl needs me."

"Is that a good idea?" asks StingRay. Frrrrrr, frrrrrr.

"Yes," says Lumphy. "I have to be tough and brave. We *all* have to be tough and brave."

Plastic bounces softly and whispers, "Brave, brave, brave!" to herself. Lumphy jumps off the windowsill and scurries to the kitchen. Plastic and StingRay follow more slowly.

"If I were lost, I know she would look for me," Lumphy tells them.

"Hello," says StingRay, following Lumphy to a cupboard, which he begins to pry open. "They went in the *car*. Bolling might be really far away."

"But they *could* be nearby," answers Lumphy.

"Won't we get wet?" StingRay is dry clean only. "Snow looks very wet." Frrrrrr, frrrrrr.

"We can't just stay home and not try to save her." Lumphy is determined. He gets a laminated place mat from the low cupboard. It has a baby stegosaurus on it. "I am a buffalo! I have thick woolly fur!" He stands on his hind legs and waves the place mat heroically over his head. "*You* don't have to get wet. *I* can save the Girl."

READY FOR MORE UNFORGETTABLE ADVENTURES
WITH LUMPHY, STINGRAY, AND PLASTIC?
OWN *all* OF THE TOYS TRILOGY!

 Meet Lumphy, StingRay, and Plastic. They all belong to the Little Girl who sleeps on the high bed. In six linked stories, the three friends face dogs, school, television commercials, the vastness of the sea, and the terrifying bigness of the washing machine.

 The Little Girl is starting to grow up, and the toys are left to fend for themselves. Together, the three best friends brave a snowstorm, rescue a mouse from the vacuum cleaner, and, of course, have a dance party.

 In this delightful prequel, readers will happily discover how the one-eared Sheep lost her ear, why StingRay is afraid of the basement—and, most importantly, how Lumphy, StingRay, and Plastic came to live with the Little Girl.

YEARLING

Turning children into readers for more than fifty years.

**Classic and award-winning literature for every shelf.
How many have you checked out?**